This edition published by Parragon Books Ltd in 2016

Parragon Books Ltd
Chartist House
15–17 Trim Street
Bath BA1 1HA, UK
www.parragon.com

ISBN 978-1-4748-5301-9

T#502013

Printed in China

Skye's Got to Fly

Bath • New York • Cologne • Melbourne • Delhi
Hong Kong • Shenzhen • Singapore

Late one afternoon, Skye was flying high over the Lookout. She was excited because her hero, stunt pilot Ace Sorensen, was coming to the air show in Adventure Bay. Skye spun and spiralled and zipped and dipped through the sky.

"Trick flying is the best!" she exclaimed.

Down on the ground, Marshall wasn't sure he agreed. The only thing he liked to fly was his kite.

Suddenly, a big gust of wind caught Marshall's kite and blew him into the air. He got tangled in the kite's string and came crashing down – right on top of Rocky!

"Sorry," Marshall said with a grin. "I guess my landing was a little rocky."

Just then, Ryder got a call on his PupPad. It was Ace Sorensen, the stunt pilot! Her plane was having engine trouble, and she needed the PAW Patrol's help to find a place to land.

"We're on it!" Ryder declared. "No job is too big and no pup is too small!"

It was starting to get dark outside. Ryder quickly called the pups to the Lookout and told them about Ace. He needed Skye's helicopter and her night-vision goggles.

"This pup's got to fly!" Skye yelped. She was eager to help her hero.

Ryder also needed Chase's spotlight and traffic cones to make a runway at Farmer Yumi's farm.

"Chase is on the case!" barked the eager German shepherd.

Finally, Ryder asked Rocky to fix Ace's plane.

"Green means go!" Rocky cheered.

The sun was setting as Skye zoomed
through the clouds in her helicopter.
She scanned the sky with her goggles
and spotted Ace's plane in the distance.
Black smoke poured out of the
engine, making it hard for Ace to see
the mountains below.

Skye pulled ahead of Ace's plane. "Follow me!" she called, and led the way to Farmer Yumi's farm.

Meanwhile, at the farm, Ryder, Chase and Rocky were preparing a runway so that Ace could land. Chase set up his orange safety cones to mark off the landing strip.

"Great job!" Ryder said. As the sky darkened, he turned to Rocky and asked if he had any old torches in his truck.

"I've got lots," Rocky replied. He quickly collected the torches. Then he and Ryder taped them to the traffic cones.

When they were done, Ryder called Skye and told her to watch for the runway lights.

"Roger that!" said Skye.

Skye zoomed through the starry night and spotted the glowing landing strip just over a hill. When she and Ace started to descend, there was a loud *BOOM!* The plane began to shake as sparks sizzled along the wing. Ace radioed to the team that she would have to parachute out of the plane!

Ryder didn't think parachuting in the dark was a good idea. He had another plan. "Ace, have you ever done the wing-walking stunt?" he asked.

"Ace is the greatest wing-walker in the whole world," Skye reported.

"Awesome!" Ryder exclaimed. He told Skye to lower her towline and safety harness.

Ace unbuckled her seat belt and carefully climbed on to the wing of her shaking plane. Skye lowered her towline and harness, and zoomed up close to Ace. The stunt pilot reached for the harness – but couldn't quite reach it.

"I've got my parachute," Ace called. "I'm going to jump!"

"No!" Skye called back. "We can do this, Ace!"
Skye lowered her helicopter and flew in as close
as she could. Ace tried again ... and this time she
grabbed the harness! She snapped herself in and
was carried through the air to Farmer Yumi's farm.

As Skye got closer to the farm, Ace radioed Ryder and asked him to track someone called Amelia.

"Sure," Ryder said. "But who's Amelia?"

"My plane," Ace replied. "Every great pilot names her plane."

Ryder tracked Amelia on his PupPad and saw that it was heading for a water landing in the bay!

"Let's find the plane and get it on to the beach before it sinks!" said Ryder.

Ryder and Chase raced to the bay, and Skye gently set Ace down at the farm. The stunt pilot unfastened her harness and waved up to the helicopter. "Thanks, Skye!" she called.

"No problem, Ace," the pilot pup called back. Then she whispered excitedly to herself, "I can't believe I saved my hero!"

Splash! Amelia sputtered, then glided to a stop in the bay. Ryder sped out to the plane on his Jet Ski and hooked a cable to its propeller. When Ryder gave the command, Chase turned on his winch and pulled Amelia to shore.

But when Ace saw her plane, she wasn't very hopeful about flying it in the air show. There was so much damage, she thought she'd need an entire team of mechanics to fix it all.

Luckily, she had the PAW Patrol!

"Reporting for duty," Rocky said.

By the glow of Chase's spotlight, Rocky screwed a
patch on to Amelia's wing. At the same time, Ryder fixed
the cockpit, while Ace checked the engine. In no time,
Skye started up the plane. The propeller began to spin,
and the engine roared. The plane was as good as new!

"I can't wait for the air show tomorrow," Skye said. Ace hopped on to one of the wings. "How would you like to see my wing-walk-and-roll trick up close?" Skye thought that sounded great!

The next day was sunny and warm, and the PAW Patrol watched the air show from Adventure Bay's beach. They cheered and waved as Amelia flew into view. Ace climbed out of the cockpit and stood on a wing. Then the plane tilted slightly, and they saw Skye smiling behind the controls.

Suddenly, Ace jumped into the air, and Skye made the plane twirl around. When the plane was level again, Ace landed back on the wing. Ryder and the pups couldn't believe their eyes. The wing-walk-and-roll trick was the most amazing stunt they'd ever seen!

"Wow!" Rocky gasped, watching Skye
zoom through the clouds. "She's so good!"
"You're all good pups," Ryder said.
The pups cheered and barked for each
other as Skye and Ace zipped overhead.

The End